THE SEA *of* TRANQUILITY

For Gina Pollinger
M.H.

For Jake
C.B.

First published in Great Britain by
HarperCollins Publishers Ltd in 1996
Text copyright © Mark Haddon 1996
Illustrations copyright © Christian Birmingham 1996
A CIP catalogue record for this title
is available from the British Library.
The author and illustrator assert the moral right to be
identified as the author and illustrator of the work.
ISBN: 0 00 198162 5
10 9 8 7 6 5 4 3 2 1

THE SEA *of* TRANQUILITY

The Sea of Tranquility

Mark Haddon
Illustrated by Christian Birmingham

Collins
An Imprint of HarperCollinsPublishers

720578

Years ago
there was a little boy
who had the solar system on his wall.

Late at night, he'd lie in bed
with Rabbit
and they'd watch the planets
spinning round the sun:
Mars, the tiny space-tomato,
Saturn, sitting in its Frisbee rings,
freezing Pluto, turning slowly in the dark,
Jupiter, Uranus, Neptune, Venus, Mercury
and Earth.

But of all the weird worlds
that whirled across his bedroom wall,
his favourite was the moon,
a small and bald and ordinary
globe of rock
that loop-the-looped
its way through outer space.

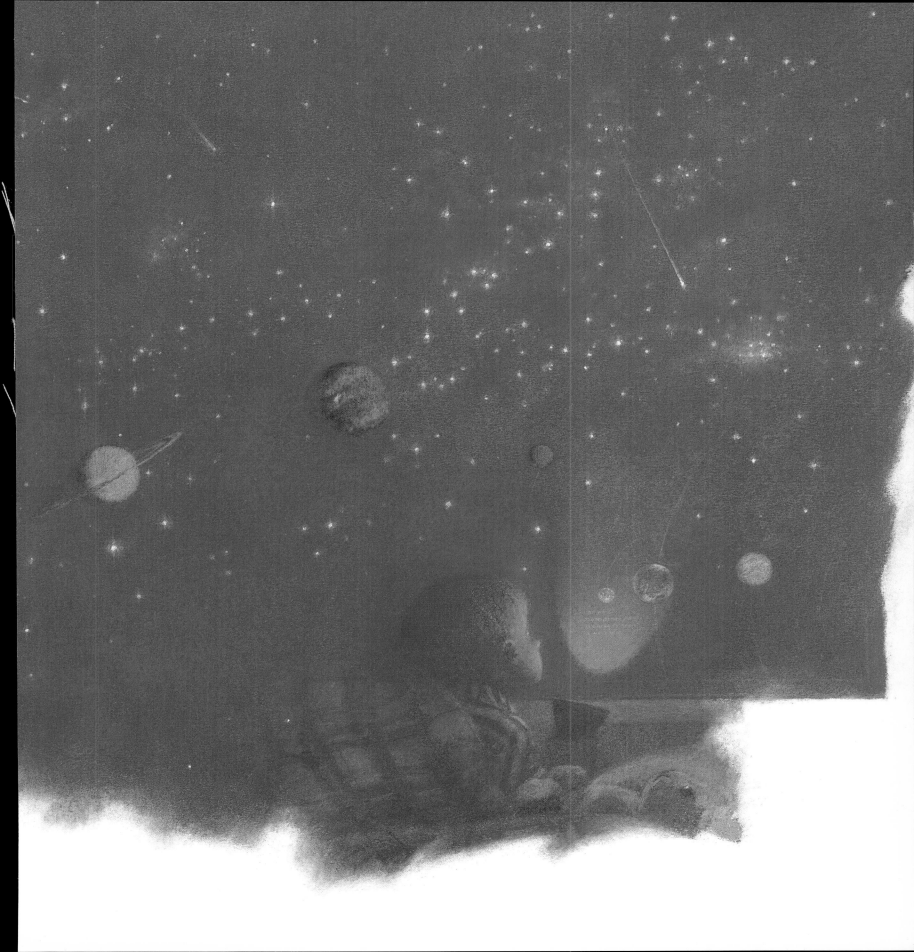

He leant across the windowsill at night
and watched the moon slide up into the sky
above the biscuit factory.

He borrowed Dad's binoculars
and gazed for hours
at the empty deserts
and the rocky mountains.

And it made him dizzy
just to think that he was looking
at another world
two hundred thousand miles away.

He got an atlas of the moon
for Christmas
and he read it
like a storybook.

He dreamed of going there,
of rocketing across the cold, black miles,
and landing on the crumbly rock.
He dreamed of visiting
the craters in the atlas,
Prosper Henry, Klaproth, Zack.
He dreamed of driving
in a fat-tyred moon-mobile,
across the Bay of Rainbows
and the Sea of Rains…

He kept a scrapbook called *The Journey to the Moon*.
Inside were photographs of rockets
taking off from Cape Canaveral
and astronauts in pumped-up suits
and fishbowl helmets,
floating in the zero gravity
around their little metal rooms.

He borrowed library books
and read how astronauts
had orbited the earth
and walked in space,
and how they'd flown around the moon itself.
And every night he hoped and hoped
that one day they would find a way to land
and walk across the tiny world
where he had dreamed of walking.

And eventually, one cloudless night,
they did.

He couldn't sleep.
Midnight had come and gone,
but he was wide awake
and standing at the window
in his dressing gown,
because two astronauts
were walking on the surface of the moon,
two hundred thousand miles
above his bedroom.

At 3 a.m.
he went downstairs
and turned the television on.
And there they were,
on the flickery screen,
bouncing slowly through the dust
in the Sea of Tranquility,
like giants in slow motion.

He stayed awake all night
and went to bed at dawn.
The sun was coming up
outside his window
and the moon was fading fast.
He fell asleep
and in his dreams
he walked with them.

That little boy was me.
I'm older now.
The solar system wall chart
fell to pieces long ago,
and Rabbit, who is older too,
no longer follows me around
but sits beside my desk
and watches while I work.

Yet still, on cloudless nights,
I sometimes sit beside my bedroom window,
staring at that tiny, distant world.

I think how cold and dark it is up there.
No wind. No clouds. No streams. No sky.
Just rocks and dust.
I think how nothing ever moves,
year after year.

And then I think of those two astronauts,
and how the prints they made
with their big boots
will still be there
tonight,
tomorrow night
and every night
for millions of years to come.